CARDED

For Marissa and Cuddles, and for Debby Grayson, who loves to dance.
– M.B.
For all my dancing friends.
– L.M.

SIMON AND SCHUSTER
First published in Great Britain in 2005 by Simon & Schuster UK Ltd
Africa House, 64-78 Kingsway, London WC2B 6AH

This paperback edition first published in 2006

Book designed by Genevieve Webster
The text for this book is set in Jerky Tash
The illustrations are rendered in collage

A CIP catalogue record for this book is available from
the British Library upon request

ISBN 0 689 87306 9
EAN 9780689873065

Printed in China
1 3 5 7 9 10 8 6 4 2

Glitter Kitty

by Mara Bergman

illustrated by Lydia Monks

SIMON AND SCHUSTER

London New York Sydney

After breakfast, Cuddles slinked through
the door of Softpaws' Salon.
"Good morning, Cuddles," Softpaws said.
"What can we do for you today?"

"I'd like a bit of colour here," said Cuddles,
waving her elegant claws, "and a bit of curl there.
Something special for tonight's dance competition.
Will you be going?"
"Of course!" said Softpaws. "And that reminds me, could you
drop this off at Rascal's Boutique on your way home?"
"With pleasure," said Cuddles.

Rascal's Boutique sold everything a cat could want.
"Why hello, Cuddles," purred Rascal.
"You're bright and early today."
"I'm getting ready for tonight's dance
competition," said Cuddles.
"Oh, and Softpaws asked me to give you this."

Suddenly she noticed a purple skirt
with pretty pink flowers.
It glowed. It flowed. Cuddles bought it at once!

As Cuddles was leaving, Rascal handed her a package.
"Would you mind dropping this off at Sugarboy's?" she said.
"With pleasure," said Cuddles. "See you later!"

"Howdy, Cuddles," Sugarboy said with
a bow. "You're looking mighty fine today."
"You're looking mighty fine yourself, Sugarboy,"
said Cuddles. "Rascal wanted you to have this."
And she gave him the package.

Suddenly she noticed the most glamorous shoes
in the world. They shimmered. They shone.
Cuddles bought them at once!
"I hope you'll save me a dance tonight," said Sugarboy.
"I'd love to," said Cuddles. "See you later!"

At home Cuddles turned the music up high
and practised all her favourite dances:

the ha-cha

and the cha-cha

the cat-trot

and the cat-twist

the mamba

and the samba

the hatty-catty

and the Meowtown Special.

Then she did them again, just to make sure.

The afternoon wore on. All that dancing wore Cuddles out!
"I'll just have a little catnap," she said,
and she slumped into her cosiest comfy chair.
ZZZZzzzzzzzz . . .

It grew late. It grew dark . . .

Cuddles woke with a start!
"Oh no!" she cried.
"THE DANCING'S ALREADY BEGUN!"

Quick – on went the purple skirt with pretty pink flowers!
Quick – on went her best velvet collar with the diamond studs!
Quick – on went her special perfume and sparkliest earrings!
Quick, quick, quick – on went the most glamorous
dance shoes in town!

Cuddles brushed her fur, tweaked her whiskers
and out the door she ran . . .

. . . and ran and ran!
"I'll never get there on time!" she cried.

Suddenly a car pulled up.
"Hop in, Cuddles!" It was Sugarboy!
"I'm running late, too. Let's go to the
dance together!"

When Sugarboy's car screeched to a stop outside the hall,
the dancing was in full swing. And when Cuddles walked
through the door, all eyes were on her.

"Look at that cool cat!" someone said. "Classy dresser!"
"Glitter kitty – wow, wow, wow!"
"Isn't she the cat's meow!"

Cuddles was all set to dance the ha-cha and the cha-cha,
the cat-trot and the cat-twist, the samba and the mamba,
the hatty-catty and, of course, the Meowtown Special.

But after only one and half numbers
the music got lower. Then it stopped.

"Ladies and Gentlemen," the compere announced.
"It's time to award the prizes."
"The prizes already?" Cuddles asked in amazement.
"How did I – how could I – did I really sleep that long?"

"Third prize goes to Softpaws!" said the compere.
All the dancers clapped.
"Second prize goes to Twinkle Toes!"
The dancers clapped even louder.

"First prize for this year's Meowtown Dance
Competition goes to . . . Cheeky Whiskers!"
Everyone clapped and cheered.
The sound was tremendous.

Cuddles was so upset she
didn't know what to say.
She didn't know where
to look.

She started to gather her things when she heard:
"Ladies and Gentlemen, this year there's a
special prize for the best-dressed dancer.

And it goes to
none other than our very own . . .
Cuddles!"

Everyone clapped and cheered and whistled!
The sound was like thunder.

Cuddles smoothed down her fur and tweaked her whiskers.
She stepped onstage and leaned into the mike.
"Thank you all very, very much. And thanks to all my friends –
I couldn't have done it without you!"

With a wave and a smile for everyone,
Cuddles took her prize.
Then she took Sugarboy's paw.
And though the competition was over,
the dancing went on
and on
and on . . .

and on!